For Ilaria, Alessia and Rob
D.M.

First published in 2022 by Nosy Crow Ltd

The Crow's Nest, 14 Baden Place, Crosby Row, London, SE1 1YW

Nosy Crow Eireann Ltd, 44 Orchard Grove, Kenmare, Co Kerry, V93 FY22, Ireland

www.nosycrow.com

ISBN 978 1 83994 496 3

Nosy Crow and associated logos are trademarks

and/or registered trademarks of Nosy Crow Ltd.

Text and illustrations copyright © David Melling 2022

The right of David Melling to be identified as the author and illustrator

of this work has been asserted.

A CIP catalogue record for this book is available from the British Library.

Printed in China

Papers used by Nosy Crow are made from wood grown in sustainable forests.

10 9 8 7 6 5 4 3 2 1

# Ruffles

and the **cosy, cosy bed**

David Melling

This is **Ruffles**.

Ruffles **loves** . . .

singing . . .

scratching . . .

eating . . .

fetching . . .

sniffing . . .

chewing . . .

digging . . .

running . . .

and sleeping.

But Ruffles **does not love** loud noises.

Loud noises make Ruffles . . .

crouch . . .

and creep . . .

and jump . . .

and skitter . . .

and scoot . . .

and stare . . .

and run . . .

and run . . .

and **run!**

There's only one thing worse than loud noises . . .

. . . and that is loud noises **at night!**

Ruffles does not like it when loud,
night noises come.

Boom . . .

bang . . .

boom . . .

flash . . .

crash . . .

flash!

Oh no!

It must . . .

be a . . .

. . . thunderstorm!

# Flash!

# Bang!

# Crash!

So Ruffles looks for somewhere to hide.

But he can't find the best place to be.

Not the towel . . .        not the box . . .        not the cupboard . . .

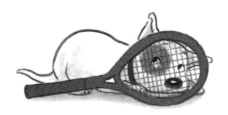  

not the racket . . .    not the laundry basket . . .    not the mat . . .

not the chair . . .        not the bucket . . .        and not the colander!

Ruffles needs somewhere quiet,
cosy and safe. Where can he go?

Suddenly, Ruffles has an idea . . .

. . . and he runs back to his very own bed.

It's quiet. It's cosy. It's safe.
It's the best place to be.

In his very . . .        own . . .        bed . . .

he has his very . . .        own . . .        cushion . . .

and his very . . .        own . . .        blankie.

Now the loud, night noises don't
seem so bad.

And before long, the thunderstorm has gone!

Ruffles loves . . .

singing . . .

scratching . . .

eating . . .

fetching . . .

sniffing . . .

chewing . . .

digging . . .

running . . .

and sleeping.

But most of all, Ruffles **loves** his very own bed.
It's the best place to be . . .

until morning!